"They're very pretty," said Mrs Noah.
Noah began to sing. "*Twinkle, twinkle,
little star!*" He was very out of tune.
He sounded like a cat yowling!

"Shh, Noah," said Mrs Noah.

"You'll frighten the animals."

"My singing isn't that bad!" said Noah.

"Oh, yes it is," smiled Mrs Noah.

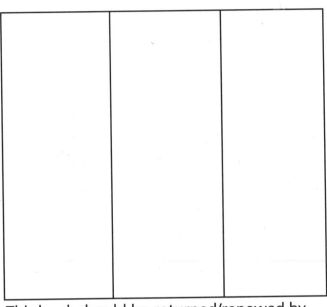

This book should be returned/renewed by the latest date shown above. Overdue items incur charges which prevent self-service renewals. Please contact the library.

Wandsworth Libraries
24 hour Renewal Hotline
01159 293388
www.wandsworth.gov.uk

L.749A (2.07)

Noah and his wife think a flood might be coming, so they have built a big boat called the Ark. They are sailing around the world to rescue the animals before it starts to rain.

Let's all go on an animal adventure!

Reading Consultant: Prue Goodwin, Lecturer in literacy and children's books

ORCHARD BOOKS
338 Euston Road, London NW1 3BH
Orchard Books Australia
Level 17/207 Kent Street, Sydney, NSW 2000

First published in 2011
First paperback publication in 2012

ISBN 978 1 40830 559 1 (hardback)
ISBN 978 1 40830 567 6 (paperback)

Text © Sally Grindley 2011
Illustrations © Alex Paterson 2011

A CIP catalogue record for this book is available from the British Library.

1 3 5 7 9 10 8 6 4 2 (hardback)
1 3 5 7 9 10 8 6 4 2 (paperback)

Printed in China

Orchard Books is a division of Hachette Children's Books,
an Hachette UK company.

Pesky
Sharks!

Written by Sally Grindley

Illustrated by Alex Paterson

ORCHARD BOOKS

It was a warm, clear night. Noah and
his wife were standing on the Ark in
their pyjamas. It was almost bedtime.
"Look at the stars twinkling,"
said Noah.

Just then, there was a loud bang on
the side of the Ark.

"What on earth was that?" said Noah.

Noah fetched his special torch with its extra long beam. He shone it over the side of the Ark.

Suddenly, a great white shark leapt out of the water. The shark grinned a wide toothy grin, then landed again with an enormous splash!

"He's got my pyjamas all wet!"

moaned Noah.

The shark leapt out of the water
again.

"He's trying to come
on board!" cried Mrs Noah.
"Tell him we're very sorry,
but we haven't got room
for fish."

Noah leant over the side of the Ark.
"Shoo, shoo!" he shouted. "We're
very sorry, but we haven't got
room for fish!"

The shark whacked his tail against the Ark and swam away.

"He's gone," said Noah.

"Phew," said Mrs Noah. "I thought he was going to wake up all the animals."

Mr and Mrs Noah went to bed.
Just as they were drifting off to sleep,
there was another bang on the side of
the Ark.

Noah looked through the cabin
window. "It's that pesky shark
again," he said. "And he's brought
a pesky friend!"

Two sharks grinned their toothy grins at them.

Noah opened the window. "Shoo!" he shouted. "We're trying to sleep." The first shark sprayed him with water.

The other whacked the Ark with his tail.

Suddenly, there was a tiny *eek!*
followed by lots of squeals.
"Now look what you've done,"
Mrs Noah grumbled. "You've woken
the mice and the guinea pigs!"

There was a loud *baaa!* followed by
lots of growls.
"And now you've woken the sheep
and the bears," grumbled Noah.

"You naughty sharks," said Mrs Noah. "We'll never get them back to sleep now."
The sharks waggled their tails cheekily.

They swam to the other side of the

Ark and banged on it again.

All over the Ark, the animals began to wake up.

WOOF! barked the dogs.

MEOW! went the cats.

GRRRR! growled the lions and tigers.

Noah and his wife ran from one part

of the Ark to another.

"Shh! Shh!" they said to the animals.

"Go back to sleep."

They tickled the foxes . . .

They stroked the rabbits . . .

They scratched the elephants . . .

They patted
the badgers . . .

They gave apples to the donkeys and zebras . . .

But every time the animals settled down, the sharks knocked on the Ark again.

"What are we going to do?" said
Noah.

"I have an idea," said Mrs Noah.

She went to a cupboard and took out
a megaphone.

"Sing to the sharks, Noah," she said.

Noah frowned, but he did as he was told. He took the megaphone and began to sing *The Animals Went In Two By Two.*

Mrs Noah put her fingers in her ears. All over the Ark, the animals howled and moaned and wailed even more loudly than before.

As soon as the sharks heard Noah,
they looked at each other in horror.
They dived back under the water and
swam away from the Ark as fast as
they could go.

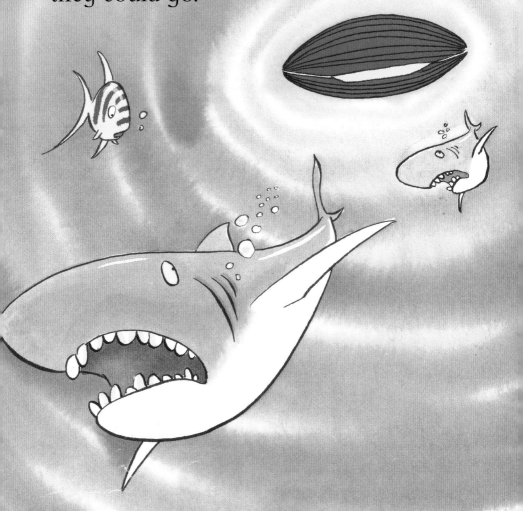

"Well done, Noah!" cried Mrs Noah
as she watched the sharks disappear.
"Your singing made them go away!"

The rest of the animals soon
settled down.

When all was quiet, Mr and
Mrs Noah went back to bed.
"Is my singing really that bad?"
asked Noah.

"Yes, Noah," smiled Mrs Noah.

"It really is!"

When all was quiet, Mr and
Mrs Noah went back to bed.
"Is my singing really that bad?"
asked Noah.

"Yes, Noah," smiled Mrs Noah.
"It really is!"

SALLY GRINDLEY · ALEX PATERSON

Crazy Chameleons!	978 1 40830 554 6
Giant Giraffes!	978 1 40830 555 3
Too-slow Tortoises!	978 1 40830 556 0
Kung Fu Kangaroos!	978 1 40830 557 7
Playful Penguins!	978 1 40830 558 4
Pesky Sharks!	978 1 40830 559 1
Cheeky Chimpanzees!	978 1 40830 560 7
Hungry Bears!	978 1 40830 561 4

All priced at £8.99

Orchard Books are available from all good bookshops, or can be
ordered from our website: www.orchardbooks.co.uk,
or telephone 01235 827702, or fax 01235 827703.